Date: 8/11/11

E MOORE
Moore, Raina,
How do you say good night? /

How Do You
Say Good Night?

To my grandma, with "lotsy" love.
—R.M.

To my own sweet ducklings, with love.
—R.L

How Do You Say Good Night?

BY RAINA MOORE

ILLUSTRATED BY ROBIN LUEBS

HarperCollinsPublishers

Ｈow do you say good night, my pup?
How do you say good night?

With a stretch and a yawn,
close my eyes until dawn.
That's how I say good night.

How do you say good night, piglet?
How do you say good night?

With a kiss and a sigh
and a sweet lullaby.
That's how I say good night.

How do you say good night, little lamb?
How do you say good night?

With a cuddle and hug
in my blanket so snug.
That's how I say good night.

How do you say good night, dear cat?
How do you say good night?

Soft pajamas, soft light,
soft pillow, just right.
That's how I say good night.

How do you say good night, sweet duckling?
How do you say good night?

In my bed, squeaky clean,
warm and safe, time to dream.
That's how I say good night.

You know how I say good night, my babe?
Do you know how I say good night?

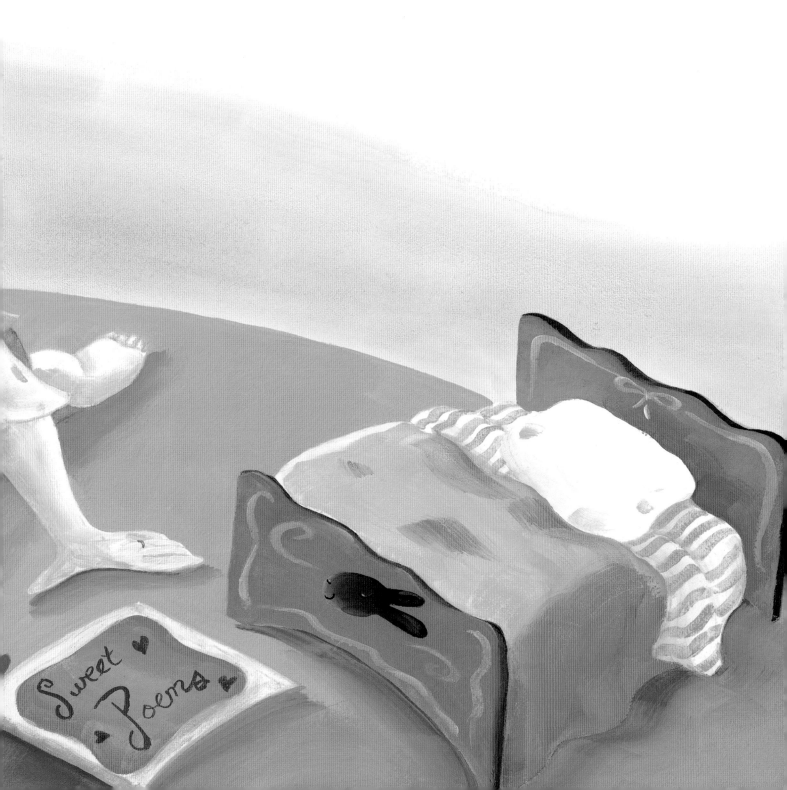

Tuck you in, snug and tight,
kiss your cheek, turn off the light.

That's how I say good night, my love.
That's how I say good night.

HOW DO YOU SAY GOOD NIGHT?
Text copyright © 2008 by Raina Moore
Illustrations © 2008 by Robin Luebs

Manufactured in China.

Library of Congress Cataloging-in-Publication Data is available.
ISBN 978-0-06-083163-9 (trade bdg.)
ISBN 978-0-06-083164-6 (lib. bdg.)

Designed by Stephanie Bart-Horvath
1 2 3 4 5 6 7 8 9 10
❖
First Edition